Health and My Body

Head Lice

by Beth Bence Reinke

PEBBLE
a capstone imprint

Pebble Explore is published by Pebble, an imprint of Capstone.
1710 Roe Crest Drive
North Mankato, Minnesota 56003
www.capstonepub.com

Library of Congress Cataloging-in-Publication Data
Names: Bence Reinke, Beth, author.
Title: Head lice / Beth Bence Reinke.
Description: North Mankato, Minnesota : Pebble, [2022] | Series: Health and my body | Includes bibliographical references and index. | Audience: Ages 5-8 | Audience: Grades K-1 | Summary: "Head lice is a common childhood problem. The bugs can spread from child to child easily, but they are just as easy to get rid of. Expertly leveled text and vibrant photos will help young readers learn about head lice and what they can do to keep the itchy insects off their heads"— Provided by publisher.
Identifiers: LCCN 2021002459 (print) | LCCN 2021002460 (ebook) | ISBN 9781663908117 (hardcover) | ISBN 9781663921017 (paperback) | ISBN 9781663908087 (pdf) | ISBN 9781663908100 (kindle edition)
Subjects: LCSH: Pediculosis—Juvenile literature
Classification: LCC RL764.P4 B46 1999 (print) | LCC RL764.P4 (ebook) | DDC 616.5/72—dc23
LC record available at https://lccn.loc.gov/2021002459
LC ebook record available at https://lccn.loc.gov/2021002460

Image Credits
Capstone Studio: Karon Dubke, 7; Shutterstock: Andrey_Popov, 19, 23, CREATISTA, 29, Daisy Daisy, 17, Dmitrii Pridannikov, 9, Golden Pixels LLC, 27, Just dance, 15, Mila_chen, 13, Monkey Business Images, 25, Pixavril, 21, Prostock-studio, 11, STUDIO GRAND WEB, Cover, Tom Wang, 5

Editorial Credits
Editor: Gena Chester; Designer: Kazuko Collins; Media Researcher: Jo Miller; Production Specialist: Tori Abraham

All internet sites appearing in back matter were available and accurate when this book was sent to press.

Printed and bound in China. 4205

Table of Contents

Bold words are in the glossary.

What Are Head Lice?

Head lice are very tiny **insects**. They live in hair on people's heads. One of the bugs is called a louse.

Head lice can live on any human head with hair. They feed on blood from the **scalp**. Lice bite the scalp to get blood. Heat from a person's skin keeps them warm.

Anyone with hair can get head lice.

People don't get lice because
of unwashed hair or dirty homes.
Anyone can get lice.

Head lice can live in hair of any color.
The hair can be curly. It can be straight.
The hair can be short or long. But head
lice don't live on animals. Pets can't
spread head lice.

You cannot get head lice from animals.

What Do Head Lice Look Like?

An adult head louse is as small as a sesame seed. They are pale gray or tan in color. They have six legs. Their six feet have claws. The claws help lice hold on to hair.

Female lice lay eggs on hair strands. The eggs are called **nits**. They are oval shaped. The female lice make glue. It makes the nits stick to hair strands. The nits hatch in about one week. The egg casings stay stuck to the hairs.

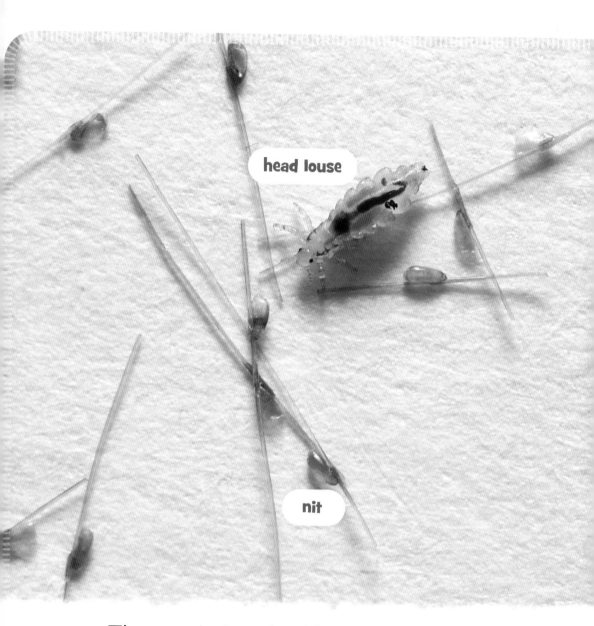

The newly hatched louse is called a **nymph**. A nymph looks like an adult louse. But it is smaller.

How Do Kids Get Head Lice?

People of any age can get head lice. But it's more common for kids. Lice go from one person's head to another. People can have head lice and not know it. They can easily spread lice to others.

Kids usually get lice from other kids. This happens when kids are close together. It happens when they share items too. Some kids hug each other. They play games side by side. Others share combs, hats, or pillows.

Sharing hair brushes can spread head lice.

How Lice Move

Head lice have no wings. They can't fly or jump. They move by crawling. A louse can live for one month on a person's head.

When kids are close together, their hair touches. Lice can crawl across hair like a bridge. That's how lice go from one head to another.

When heads touch, lice can travel from one to the other.

Lice can crawl onto things heads touch. They can crawl inside a hat. They may get on combs or brushes. Then someone else puts on the hat or uses the comb. The lice crawl onto that person's hair. Now that person has lice.

Sharing winter hats can spread head lice.

Signs of Head Lice

Your head may itch when you have lice. You might feel a tickle on your head. That means the insects are moving. But your head can itch for different reasons. Your scalp might itch from **dandruff**. A rash can also cause itchy skin. Scratchy fabric or hats might make you itchy too.

It might be hard to sleep if you have lice. Head lice are more active in the dark. The bugs bite your scalp. Their **saliva** is what makes you itch. You may want to scratch your head. But scratching your scalp a lot can cause sores.

An itchy head is a sign of head lice.

If your head is itchy, tell a trusted adult. You can tell a parent. Or go to the school nurse. A trusted adult can check your head for lice.

Adults can look at your scalp. They might see red dots from the bites. Or they might see the lice crawling.

Lice are often found near the ears and behind the neck. But lice are not easy to see in hair. They don't like light. They hide under hair where it's dark. They can crawl really fast.

Adults can look for nits. Nits are easier to find. The eggs stick to hair. They don't move.

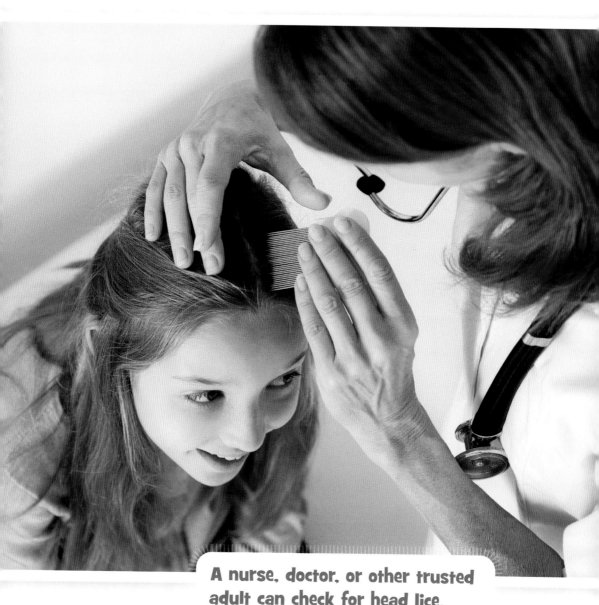

A nurse, doctor, or other trusted adult can check for head lice.

Treating Head Lice

If you have head lice, don't worry. Treating lice gets rid of them. A trusted adult can do the treatment at home. You don't need to go to the doctor.

The treatment has two parts. The first part is a special shampoo. A parent washes your hair with it. The shampoo has medicine in it. It kills the lice.

A special shampoo gets rid of head lice.

The shampoo does not kill nits. If they hatch, new lice come out. The second part of treatment is getting rid of the nits.

A trusted adult must pick out the nits. A nit comb works for this job. The comb has metal teeth. The teeth are very close together. They catch the tiny nits.

Sometimes there are lots of nits. Combing them out can take a long time. Try to be patient. All the nits need to come out. If any are left, new lice will hatch.

A special comb helps get nits out of your hair.

Cleaning Things at Home

Head lice can be on anything hair touches. They can fall on the sofa or carpet. They can crawl onto pillow cases, sheets, and stuffed animals. They can get on clothes too.

Washing things kills lice. Ask a trusted adult for help. Put clothes and bedding into a washing machine. Use hot water and laundry soap. Dry everything in the dryer. Use the hottest setting.

Clean your brushes and combs. Wash them in hot soapy water. Wash hair accessories too.

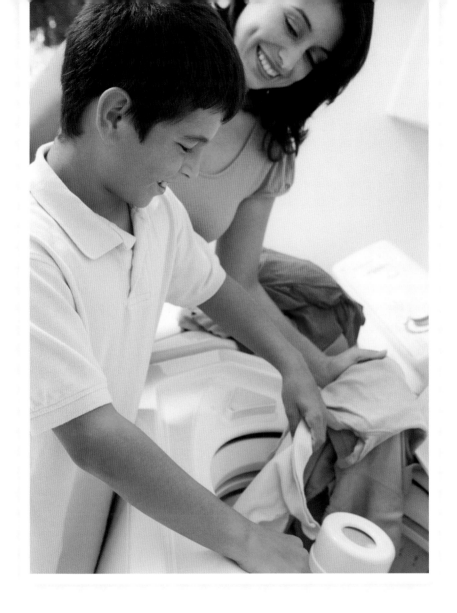

Lice may get on things you can't wash. Vacuuming also gets rid of lice. You can vacuum rugs and furniture, and throw pillows.

Stay Away, Head Lice!

No one tries to get head lice. Lice spread by accident. But there are ways to avoid getting them.

Remember, lice can spread from head to head. If your friend has lice, keep a safe distance. Don't put your heads together or hug.

Most of the time, sharing things with friends is nice. But sharing some things can spread lice. Don't use someone else's brushes or hair ties. Never put on other people's hats. Wash new hats before wearing them.

Don't share pillows at sleepovers. Take along a pillow from home. Use your own sleeping bag too.

School nurses check kids' heads at school sometimes for head lice. You can help too. Ask a trusted adult to check your head at home if you think you might have lice. Remember, you are in charge of your health.

Head lice can spread from sharing
sleeping bags or pillows at a sleepover.

Glossary

dandruff (DAN-druhf)—white flakes of dead skin

head louse (HED LOUS)—an insect that lives in hair on the scalp

insect (IN-sekt)—a small animal with a hard outer shell, six legs, three body sections, and two antennae

nit (NIT)—a louse egg

nymph (NIMF)—a baby louse

saliva (suh-LY-vuh)—the clear liquid in the mouth

scalp (SKALP)—the skin that covers the top of the head where hair grows

Read More

Borgert-Spaniol, Megan. *All About Head Lice.* Minneapolis: Abdo, 2018.

Dickmann, Nancy. *What You Need to Know About Head Lice.* North Mankato, MN: Capstone Press, 2016.

Sanchez, Anita. *Itch!: Everything You Didn't Want to Know About What Makes You Scratch.* Boston: Houghton Mifflin Harcourt, 2018.

Internet Sites

HeadLice.org: Just for Kids
headlice.org/kids/index.htm

KidsHealth: What Are Head Lice?
kidshealth.org/en/kids/lice.html

PestWorldforKids: Lice
pestworldforkids.org/pest-guide/lice/

Index